Meg Cabot is the aut[...] young adults, including [...] cessful *The Princess Diari*[...] *Nicola and the Viscount* and *Victoria and the Rogue*, as well as several books for adult readers. Meg currently lives in New York City with her husband and one-eyed cat, Henrietta, and says she is still waiting for her real parents, the king and queen, to restore her to her rightful throne.

There is a Walt Disney Pictures feature film based on *The Princess Diaries*, and a second one is in production.

Visit Meg Cabot's website at
www.megcabot.co.uk

The PRINCESS FILES

Meg Cabot

Illustrated by Nicola Slater

MACMILLAN CHILDREN'S BOOKS

First published 2004 by Macmillan Children's Books
a division of Macmillan Publishers Limited
20 New Wharf Road, London N1 9RR
Basingstoke and Oxford
www.panmacmillan.com

Associated companies throughout the world

ISBN 0 330 42629 X

3 5 7 9 8 6 4 2

A CIP catalogue record for this book is available from
the British Library.

Printed and bound in China.

To princesses everywhere,
past, present and pretend

Thank you to those of who you contributed
to this book, princesses all:
Beth Ader, Jennifer Brown, Barb Cabot, Sarah Davies,
Michael Jaffe, Laura Langlie, Nicola Slater, and especially
royal consort Benjamin Egnatz, a true prince

Lilly

Michael

Mia

Lars

Grandmere

Prince Phillippe

Tina

Hank

Paolo

Sebastiano

Shameeka

René

Kenny

Lana

Josh

Fat Louie

CONTENTS

III. **Style Princesses**

Hair and make-up guru Paolo and fashionisto Sebastiano discuss principessas whose royal wardrobes have profoundly impacted on the world. Also: a special guest appearance by Cousin Hank Thermopolis.

✦ *From Marie Antoinette's rosy cheeks to Princess Jasmine's halter-neck top, royal style relies on more than just a crown. Paolo and Sebastiano explain how.*

IV. **Mrs Princesses**

Tina Hakim Baba names princesses who only became princesses because they were lucky enough to marry a prince.

✦ *From Princess Diana to Mia's own Grandmere, Tina examines the phenomenon of commoners who scored royal titles. And princes.*

V. Power Princesses 73

Renowned social activist Lilly Moscovitz on
princesses who wielded mighty sceptres.

* *From Cleopatra and her fatal asp to Elizabeth the
Virgin Queen, these royals refused to merely sit
pretty on their thrones.*

VI. Action Princesses 97

Royal Consort Michael Moscovitz
reflects upon his ideal princess . . .
and, surprisingly, it is not Princess Leia.

* *Michael tells all (or at least his thoughts on
heroines in tiaras, that is).*

I. Introduction

All I Need to Know I Learned from Princesses

By Her Royal Highness Princess Amelia Mignonette Grimaldi Thermopolis Renaldo

Imagine it: one day you're just this normal ninth-grader with too-big feet and too-small breasts, whose biggest concern is passing Algebra and/or whether or not your best friend's hottie brother knows you're alive. The next thing you know, you're a princess. Suddenly, everybody around you is talking tiaras and tariffs. But you're still all, 'What's on the WB tonight?'

Like adolescence isn't bad enough, with the

1

zits and the bad-hair days and the nobody-understands-me thing. Try taking all that and throwing a big ermine cape over it (except not, because wearing fur is wrong unless you are like an Eskimo and really need mink to stay alive in the sub-arctic temperatures or whatever).

Fortunately my grandmother – formally known as the Dowager Princess Clarisse Renaldo, or, as I simply call her, Grandmere – stepped in with the whole princess-lessons idea. True, my chance of ever taking part in after-school extra-curriculars is totally shot, on account of how I have to go to Grandmere's every afternoon to learn how to pour tea and say, 'I don't prefer any more finger sandwiches, thank you,' in seven different languages.

But while I'm still not exactly sure about the whole posture thing and how much of a tip to leave the hotel manicurist in Beijing, one thing I have got down is the fact that I am not the world's first – or even its last – princess.

And just knowing that I'm not alone – that there are people who endured exactly what I'm going through – is like such a major comfort, I can't even tell you. Read on to find out about other princesses – past, present and pretend – who made major impacts on society, and what we, as princesses in training, can learn from their triumphs and mistakes.

II. Perfect Princesses

Princesses Who Showed Grace Under Pressure

A Note from Princess Mia Thermopolis

Grandmere says the only way we as a society can learn from our mistakes is to scrutinize them carefully, and swear never to repeat them. I guess this would explain why I'm stuck in princess lessons with her every single weekday from four to six.

Not surprisingly, Grandmere thinks SHE's the most suitable person to consult about royal role models. She says in her day, young women did not look up to scantily clad and weapon-wielding princesses such as Xena and 'that other one, the one with the robots and the buns on the sides of her head' (!!!!!!), but to royals such as Princess Margaret and Isabella of Spain.

And though Grandmere says that there are any number of highly memorable princesses she would recommend that I emulate, she always adds, 'Though I feel I can say – without flattering myself, which would be highly unprincesslike – that I'm probably your most suitable role model, seeing as how I  have always done my best to remain conscious of the duties of the crown . . . the primary one of which is to remain, at all times, a good example to the impressionable youth of today.'

Whatever! I suppose it is setting a good example to smoke a pack a day and swill down about a zillion Sidecars before breakfast.

On the other hand, it's true you hardly ever read about Grandmere in the *National Enquirer*. She is the epitome of discretion. At least, outside the confines of the palace. Inside, all bets are off.

Elizabeth, the late Queen Mother

By Grandmere, Dowager Princess of Genovia,
Grandmother to Mia Thermopolis
[with commentary by Mia Thermopolis]

The late Queen Mother of Great Britain – often
vulgarly referred to as the Queen Mum – is a perfect example of a princess who comported herself

with grace and dignity throughout her long life. The mother of the longest-ruling sovereign in British history, one of 'Queen Bess's' most notable contributions to the throne was her insistence that her family stay together during World War II. Rather than shipping her two young daughters, the Princesses Elizabeth and Margaret, to safety in the countryside, as many London parents were doing, the Queen kept the girls at her side in the Palace . . . a palace which was frequently strafed by Luftwaffe gunfire and even, on several occasions, bombed by the Nazi horde.

Her Majesty refused to be daunted by this senseless onslaught, and bravely visited her less fortunate subjects, commoners whose own homes had been blown to smithereens, in the very craters in which their beds once stood, offering tips as to how the damage might be repaired while never getting so much as a smudge on her crisp cotton gloves. Indomitable and cheerful throughout her husband's reign, the Queen Mother is a perfect example of a regent who showed grace under pressure . . . and always while wearing a delightful confection of a chapeau.

Um. OK. The part about the Nazis is cool.

Grandmere's Random Act of Princess:

Be like the Queen Mother: brighten the day of someone less fortunate than yourself by going to visit him or her while wearing a pair of white gloves and a charming hat with an adorable matching clutch bag. The poor invalid will be cheered by the effort you made to look your best.

Princesses Elizabeth and Margaret

Like their mother, the young Windsor princesses showed remarkable character during their teen years, despite living in near constant fear of being murdered in their beds by an invading Nazi scourge. The brave princesses cheerfully assisted their mother in rolling bandages for the Royal Air Force, and wore cunning little khaki Wren uniforms, just like all the other British girls who chose to volunteer to stop the tyrannical oppression of the Axis powers by running canteens and casino nights for war-weary British soldiers. Through it all they had to endure not only the knowledge that they might at any moment be blown to kingdom come, but also rationing, as things like sugar and – perish the thought! – silk stockings were scarce and had to be saved for the war effort.

Perhaps most horrifying of all, during the height of the war, the princesses were forced to bathe in a *maximum* of only four inches of tepid water, and only *once* daily. I have it on certain authority that their mother put tape inside the tub to indicate the level the water was not to exceed. Such privations are doubtless why the two princesses grew into such responsible and respectable women, well capable of bearing the aristocratic mantle thrust upon them so early in life.

That's nothing. During water shortages in the summer time here in NYC, the mayor's office issues directives about how often you are supposed to flush the toilet. Having to endure something like that is what I call character building. In fact, I might even be scarred for life.

Mia's Random Act of Princess:

Be like Princesses Elizabeth and Margaret: grow a Victory garden! You don't need a garden to do it, either. Plant basil and parsley seeds in cups of soil and place them on your window sill. Snip off leaves when they are grown to add to salads, pasta dishes, even pizzas! This way, if an invading force ever enters YOUR city, and supply lines to your local grocery store are cut off, you'll still have the ability to make tasty treats for your friends.

Alice, Princess Andrew of Greece

Perhaps best known as the mother of Prince Philip, the royal consort of Queen Elizabeth II of England, Alice was a dear friend who ministered to the sick in Greek hospitals and soup kitchens, and who sheltered a Jewish family during the Holocaust (for which she was posthumously given the title Righteous Among the Nations, an honour Oskar Schindler also received). A gracious lady and superlative hostess, Alice was everything one would expect from someone with the title Her Royal Highness.

Whatever! My dad gave me the real scoop on Princess Alice: when Czar Nicholas of Russia got a little too carried away, pelting Alice with rice at her 1903 wedding to Prince Andrew, she got him to cut it out by grabbing a shoe and whacking him on the head with it a few times. Way to go, Alice!

Mia's Random Act of Princess:

Be like Alice: install a dartboard on the back of your bedroom door. During your spare moments from homework and good works amongst the poor, practise your hand–eye coordination. You never know when good aim might come in handy.

Wu Zetian

For nearly a century during the Tang Dynasty, though hardly anyone seems to know it, a woman was Emperor of China. Her name was Wu Zetian, and she rose well above her birth rank, which was that of a lowly peasant, by becoming a princess upon marrying the Emperor's son. After her husband, who soon inherited the throne, suffered a stroke, Princess Wu stepped in and assumed the administrative duties of government, eventually being named Empress.

By all reports Empress Wu was a benevolent and kind ruler, doing much to elevate the status of women in Chinese society particularly women belonging to her own family. Empress Wu also siphoned money away from the military and spent it on education reform. She also lowered taxes, an act which rarely makes a regent unpopular with her people.

In Genovia, there are no taxes. That's because the amount of money the tourists lose gambling in Genovian casinos every year exceeds the gross national debt by several hundred million. Gambling can be very addictive, you know, which is why when I take over the throne I intend to offer Gamblers Anonymous meetings right in the palace. Only don't tell Grandmere.

Mia's Random Act of Princess:

Be like Wu: join your student council. Vote for more spending on arts and sciences than on athletics, except for the girls' teams. When male student council members accuse you of being partisan, say, 'What's your point?'

Anastasia

The youngest daughter of Tsar Nicholas II, Anastasia was a lively and pretty girl, who lived happily with her parents and older sisters and younger brother . . . until tragedy struck, that is. Tragedy came to the Romanovs in the form of Rasputin, a so-called holy man who appeared to 'cure' Anastasia's little brother of haemophilia, an incurable blood disorder. The Russian people were a little more sceptical of Rasputin's claims, and the royal family's faith in him shook the Russian people's faith in the Romanovs. Soon, revolution occurred, and the Romanovs were cruelly set upon and shot in cold blood – although it took longer to kill Anastasia and her sisters, because they had sewn the family jewels into their corsets, and the bullets kept bouncing off them.

Which should be a lesson to us all: never listen to the advice of charlatans.*

The body of Anastasia and her brother, incidentally, were never found, leading many to believe that the youngest Romanov daughter might still be alive today.**

*Also, it is probably a bad idea to wear bras made out of diamonds.
**If Anastasia is still alive, can I just say, RUN! Get out now while the going is good! Don't let them find you and force YOU to take princess lessons every day, like me! Save yourself!

Mia's Random Act of Princess:

Be like Anastasia: be kind to your younger siblings. Take them to the park or to a movie. You never know whether you might need to use one of them as a human shield in the event of an assassination attempt.

Rosagunde

Princess Rosagunde is perhaps the most important woman in Genovian history, being, in fact, the country's founder. It was Rosagunde who fought against the Visigoth warlord Albion. Albion was a dreadful young man who took it upon himself to descend upon Italy in the year 568AD and kill everyone who stood in his path to the throne. One of these unfortunates was poor Rosagunde's father, a general in the true king of Italy's army.

After dispatching the brave general, Albion declared himself king, and when his gaze fell upon fair Rosagunde, he decided then and there to make her his queen.

Most young women, of course, would have been thrilled at the prospect of ruling a country the size of Italy, but Rosagund was still understandably upset over the foul murder of her father. It didn't help matters that, on her wedding night to Albion, he attempted to force her to drink wine from her father's skull in a sign of fealty to him, the new king.

Rosagunde had no choice but to do as he asked, but she got justice the old-fashioned way by strangling Albion in his sleep later that night with her long, flaxen braid.

The king of Italy was of course so grateful to Rosagunde for ridding his country of Albion's horrid presence that he made her princess of Genovia, a small strip of beautiful land along the Mediterranean coast, over which she ruled wisely and well for many, many years.

I can only hope that in the face of such hardship I will show as much bravery as my ancestress Rosagunde. So far, considering the whole flunking

Algebra thing, it's not looking too good. Were a foreign invader to kill my father and force me to drink wine from his skull, I would have a hard time strangling him with my hair, because it is still only chin-length. I'm really trying to grow it out, though, just in case.

Grandmere's Random Act of Princess:

Be like Rosagunde: while it is often the best strategy to kill your enemies with kindness (see page 93) there might come a time when your life – or maidenhood – is in actual peril. This is why a passing knowledge of krav maga or karate is highly suggested for today's modern young princesses.

Aleta, Queen of the Misty Isles

Amelia insists that I include a fictional princess or two in addition to the 'real life' ones I've mentioned. While I find it quite ludicrous to suggest that there are important tips on asserting one's royalness to be learned from a fictional character, I will admit that, for every Sunday for almost as long as I can remember, I have been mildly impressed by the regal dignity with which the wife of Prince Valiant, the chivalrous gallant of the comics pages, comported herself.

And it certainly cannot have been easy, attempting to live like a noblewoman in an era during which there were no foundation garments or even mirrors. In addition to which, Aleta seems to have a marked preference for togas . . . very unflattering to all but the most statuesque of women.

However, it must be admitted that Valeta and

Karen, Valiant and Aleta's twin daughters, have also proved courageous, if somewhat romantically challenged, princesses. Except for a few lapses, during which one or the other of these girls has traipsed off after their father or brother, disguised as a boy with a sword in his hand, they have shown a good sense that many 'real life' princesses today are markedly lacking. In all, I find that the Queen of the Misty Isles and her daughters make for fine, if fictional, examples of royal grace.

The girl who played Aleta in the 'Prince Valiant' movie was the same girl who plays Isabel on 'Roswell'. Also, Aleta and Valiant's son, Prince Arn, is married to a totally cool princess, Maeve, the daughter of King Arthur's creepy son, Prince Mordred.

But Maeve can't help who her father is — and at least Mordred is better than Darth Vader. Anyway, Maeve is a dog whisperer, just like the guy Robert Redford played in that movie, only with dogs, not horses. Personally, I believe I am a cat whisperer, since Fat Louie will do almost anything I say. Except, you know, get me a soda from the kitchen when I'm busy at the computer. But that's just because he doesn't have opposable thumbs.

Grandmere's Random Act of Princess:

Be like Aleta: don't dismiss the awkward, 'geeky' boys in your class. It's entirely possible that one of them might discover he is actually a long-lost prince whose parents were forced to give him up for his own protection . . . just like Valiant!

The Princess and the Pea

While many mock the story of *The Princess and the Pea* for portraying a heroine who is so absurdly sensitive that she can feel something as small as a pea through a twenty-foot pile of mattresses, I do feel it ought to be pointed out that by pea, the narrators of this tale are not referring to the soggy things you and I frequently find upon our plates in restaurants. Indeed not! Such a pea would, of course, be crushed beneath the weight of all those mattresses, and rendered undetectable to anyone, even a princess.

The narrators in this case mean an uncooked, dry pea. Of course only the most  sensitive of us would be able to feel such a pea beneath so much padding. But feel it we would. Because princesses, besides being used to the finer things in life, are extremely sensitive creatures . . . incredibly giving and uncomplaining, but still: very, very sensitive. You will note that the princess in the story of *The Princess and the Pea* was quite reluctant to share with the queen the truth about her restless night . . . she did not want her hostess to feel bad after having offered such kind hospitality.

This is as it should be, of course. A princess sensitive enough to feel a pea through a dozen or more pieces of bedding ought also be sensitive enough not to insult those who've shown her kindness.

And that, if you ask me, is the REAL meaning behind the story of *The Princess and the Pea*. Yes, we princesses are sensitive to the slightest discomfort . . . but also to the smallest slight, and we behave accordingly, in order to spare our subjects the pain we ourselves are feeling.

Whatever. I keep my diary under my mattress at night, and I have never had an uncomfortable night's sleep because of it. And my diary is quite lumpy, considering all the pictures of Michael I've glued into it.

Grandmere's Random Act of Princess:

Be like the princess in *The Princess and the Pea*: be sure to get eight hours of sleep every night, if not more. A princess must be well rested in order to properly govern her people. Late-night partying, while all right for heiresses, pop stars and super-models, has no place in the life of those aspiring to one day rule the throne.

III. Style Princesses

Princesses Whose Fashion Finesse
Had a Profound Impact on the World

A Note from Princess Mia

Princesses have traditionally had a lot of impact on the world of fashion, even all the way back in olden times. When Queen Elizabeth the First dyed her hair red, so did all the ladies in her court.

And when Josephine, the wife of the Emperor Napoleon, started wearing these high-waisted dresses to hide her pregnancy, so did everybody else, not just in France, but all over Europe (and most of them weren't even pregnant!).

But I guess it sort of depends on the princess, since so far I haven't exactly seen this burgeoning demand around the world for Doc Marten combat boots, or anything. But hey, who knows, soon flat-chestedness and triangular-shaped hair might totally come into style!

Queen Victoria

By Paolo, Royal Hairstylist and Cosmetician, and
Sebastiano, Fashion Designer and Wardrobe Consultant
[with commentary by Mia Thermopolis]

Queen Victoria was a principessa who had the most profound impact on fashion during her more than sixty years on the English throne.

Anyone who has seen the movie classicos *Gone with the Wind* or *The King and I* knows how important the hoop skirt was to both those stories Scarlett's kept getting caught on things, and Anna's . . . well, the sight of her dancing with Yul Brynner would not have been nearly as impressive if she'd been wearing one of Empress Josephine's high-waisted muslin frocks, no?

When the Principessa Victoria step on to the throne, all over England, small feet, they become the rage! Because the Principessa Victoria, she have the tiny feet.

And because she is so small, the Principessa Victoria keeps ordering her skirts to be made wider and wider, so she looks more impressive in the throne room, no? Soon everyone everywhere is wearing skirts so wide, they hardly fit through the door!

Soon a style of dress is named just for her – the Princess dress, still around today! The bustle

eventually replaced the hoop skirt in popularity, but only after the Principessa, she so saddened by death of her husband Albert, she retire to the castle and won't come out for no one. When she die, people all over the world, they cry too, because who gonna tell them what to wear now, eh?

~Paolo~

Queen Vic take ver good care of her skin. She always use the soap and water and ex with sponge. That's why she look so good.*

~Sebastiano~

* Because English is Sebastiano's second language, he sometimes forgets the second syllables of words. Here he means:
Queen Victoria took very good care of her skin, and exfoliated with a sponge.

She also had nine children and extended the British Empire from India all the way to Melbourne. But who cares about that?

A popular prank that my cousin Hank liked to play, back where he lived in Indiana, was to call up the local drugstore and ask them if they have Prince Albert in the can. Then when they say they do, you're supposed to go, 'Well, hadn't you better let him out?' Prince Albert is apparently some form of chewing tobacco. He was also Queen Victoria's husband, the one she had all the kids with. Whatever. It can get pretty boring in Indiana.

Mia's Random Act of Princess:

Be like Victoria: invite your friends over for tea. Do the British thing and put milk in your tea instead of lemon or honey. Serve tiny cucumber sandwiches on white bread with the crusts cut off. Totally vegan AND delicious!

Principessa Caroline of Monaco and Her Sister, Principessa Stephanie

Caroline and Stephanie, daughters of Prince Rainier of Monaco and Principessa Grace (formerly Grace Kelly, the movie actress), are molto bella, just like their mamma. They have their mother's loveliness, just like they have their father's Mediterranean hot temper and love for the champagne, no? Sought after by play-boys all over Europe and beyond for their faces and fortunes, the little principessas have always been the most popular of the European royals. The Principessa Stephanie, she is even the model for the short time!

The principessas, they marry, to the race-car drivers and the speed-boat drivers and even to the bodyguards! Today the principessas, they are raising their own little princes and principessas, who look as bella as their mammas and their grandmamma!

~Paolo~

The Prin Car and Steph have bods like mods and can wear any. With their tans they look esp good in white or black.*

~Sebastiano~

* What Sebastiano seems to be trying to say here is:
The Princesses Caroline and Stephanie have bodies like models and can wear anything. With their tans they look especially good in white or black.

But let's examine what's really important here:

ONE OF THEM MARRIED HER BODYGUARD??? Big fat EW! I would so never marry one of my bodyguards. I mean, for one thing, they are all too old . . . and in Lars's case at least, so not my type. I mean, in his spare time, Lars likes to go boar hunting. BOAR HUNTING.

Need I say more?

Mia's Random Act of Princess:

Be like Princesses Caroline and Stephanie: on the first warm, sunny Saturday of spring, spend time outside in order to get rid of your pasty winter complexion. Due to the destruction of the ozone layer, though, you should be sure to wear plenty of sunscreen. There's nothing appealing about burnt princesses!

Marie Antoinette

Poor Marie! So misunderstood! She only wants to make things pretty – who doesn't? And she try so hard, married to that little pot-belly Dauphin. He love her so, he build her a little village of her own, so she can pretend to be the milkmaid! Soon all of the royals in France are pretending to be the milkmaids. Like Little Bo Beep, these milkmaid principessas look!

Only the real milkmaids, they not so happy about it, no? Because they have to do all the work.

Still, nothing bring out the rosy cheeks like exercise, and what better exercise is there, than bringing in the milk?

~Paolo~

Milk! It does the bod good!*
~Sebastiano~

*I believe Sebastiano is trying to say that milk does the body good.

It is very hard for me to keep all these princesses straight in my head, especially during the frequent pop quizzes Grandmere springs on me during our princess lessons. So I wrote this poem about Marie Antoinette, to keep her from getting confused with everybody else:

There once was a great queen of France,
who spent millions on wine and romance.
The peasants complained,
'cause the money had been drained
from their purses and seats of their pants.

The queen, she ignored their complaining,
and for most of the time she was reigning
she closed palace doors,
called the peasants, 'Such bores!'
and there was no fireworks or parading.

Till, 'Your Majesty, Ma'am,' said a squire,
'of your rule the peasants do tire.
They have nothing to eat —
no bread and no meat
they're setting the palace on fire!'

To which the queen cried, 'Oh, for heaven's sake —
why do you quiver and quake?
If no bread's in the pantry, and
meat is so scanty,
why don't we let them eat cake?'

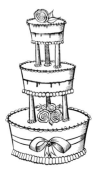

Mia's Random Act of Princess:

Be like Marie: remember the little people. Be kind to food-service industry workers, and tip well! Princesses are always gracious to waiting staff.

Principessa Marcella Borghese

Principessa Marcella Borghese, the Duchesa di Bomarzo, was the legendary beauty who founded the Princess Marcella Borghese cosmetics company in the sixties . . . during which time she was often seen wearing Pucci, the Abercrombie and Fitch of Italia. The principessa, she love the spa treatments: she introduced the idea of the mud bath to the Western world, formerly ignorant of its therapeutic beauty benefits.

Poor Principessa Marcella died in Switzerland and is buried in the Borghese family crypt in Rome, leaving behind twin sons. But her beauty legacy, it lives on forever!

~Paolo~

The Prin Borghese, for all we know, may still

be look for prin of their own.*

~Sebastiano~

*I believe what Sebastiano is trying to say here is:
The Princes Borghese may still be looking for principessas of their own.

Forgive me if I don't get excited. For one thing, I've already found my prince. And for another, can these guys really be any match for Princes William and Harry? I mean, with competition like that, why even try?

Mia's Random Act of Princess:

Be like Marcella: think royal red! Try a shade of lipstick you normally wouldn't wear – fiery crimson or flaming scarlet. Practise kissing on napkins. Someday when you're famous those napkins will sell for tons of money on eBay.

Princess Jasmine

Jasmine, the principessa from the movie of *Aladdin*, she does more than rescue that bambino with the flying carpet from his own wretched poverty and obscurity. She single-handedly reintroduces the halter-neck top back into fashion! Si! After it is seemingly dropped from the imagination of designers everywhere (no offence to Señor Sebastiano). That jewel in her navel? It also does much to fan the flames of the pierced-belly-button craze. Bella Jasmine!

~Paolo~

Grazie, Jas!*
~Sebastiano~

*I think Sebastiano is trying to say:
Thank you, Jasmine.

OK, I will admit it: I once dressed as Princess Jasmine for Hallowe'en. But since it was cold out, my mom made me wear long johns beneath my see-through harem pants, which fully spoilt the effect.

Mia's Random Act of Princess:

Be like Jasmine: make anklets like Jasmine's for yourself and your friends. Wear them every single moment of the day, even in the shower. Whoever's anklet falls off first will be the one to become betrothed to the hot ruler of a foreign land.

Princess Ariel

The little mermaid, who gives up her beautiful singing voice in order to get the legs and be near the man she loved? Who can forget her? Ciao, Ariel, we love you! How can we forget her, when she brings back to popularity the very famous shell bra? Not since Botticelli's Venus do we see this bra (well, her hair covers up the bra in the painting, but we Italians, we know it's there). Brava, Ariel, for bringing back the bra!

~Paolo~

Ariel, her hair is love, with the nat curls and deep au col.* And her tail is quite nice, too.

~Sebastiano~

*I believe Sebastiano is complimenting Ariel's lovely hair, with its natural curls and deep auburn colour.

I don't think I've got enough upstairs to fit into a shell bra, if you know what I mean. This is why I never dressed as Ariel for Hallowe'en. Also my mom wouldn't let me, since she says Ariel is a feminist's nightmare for turning her back on her own species in her effort to secure a man and, besides which, what are her and Prince Eric's babies going to look like anyway? Tadpoles? Also, in the non-Disney version of this story, the prince fully marries some other chick. So then Ariel kills herself. Nice fairy tale, huh????

Mia's Random Act of Princess:

Be like Ariel: join the swimming team! Swimming is an excellent form of cardiovascular exercise. Just make sure you wear a swimming cap, so the chlorine doesn't damage your hair. Nothing looks worse than a tiara on green tresses.

Corn Princess of Versailles, Indiana

Special Guest Supplement by Hank Thermopolis,
Male Model and Cousin to Princess Mia

The most stylish princess I ever saw was my ex-girlfriend Amber Grubb, who was Corn Princess of Versailles, Indiana, three years running. In case you aren't too familiar with corn princesses, let me tell you, they are a very special kind of princess. For one thing, they ain't – I mean, aren't – born into the position like Cousin Mia was.

Heck, no! To be Corn Princess, you got to be ELECTED. And it ain't – I mean, isn't – easy getting elected Corn Princess of Versailles, Indiana, because the competition is something fierce.

Corn princesses don't just got to have beauty and talent, though. They got to answer some pretty tough questions during the final judging phase. Like, What is the Indiana state bird? Some of you might say the turkey buzzard, because you see their dang carcasses lying by the side of the road so often. But no, the correct answer is the cardinal. And the Indiana state flower? No, it ain't – I mean, isn't – ragweed, though you see that a lot by the side of the road, too. It's the frangipani! Don't ask me what a frangipani looks like though. Don't think I ever seen one. Sure as heck Mamaw didn't have none of them in her rock garden . . .

Anyways, those are just a few of the important things the Corn Queen of Versailles, Indiana, has to know. And that doesn't even include all the stuff she's got to know AFTER she gets crowned, like how to cut the ribbon at the grand opening of the new Kroger Sav-On or whatnot. It takes a real special person to be a princess. We all know that.

But it takes an EXTRA SPECIAL person to be a corn princess.

And don't you forget it.

51

Sadly, I don't think I'll be able to. Ever.

Mia's Random Act of Princess:

Be like Amber: memorize facts about the community in which you live, such as your state flower and bird. Impress your friends and family with your extensive knowledge of local trivia. You never know when it could come in handy. Like as extra credit on a report or something.

IV. Mrs Princesses

Princesses Who Only Became Princesses Because They Married a Prince, But We Love Them Anyway

A Note from Princess Mia Thermopolis

From the dawn of time, millions and millions of women have dreamed of being swept up and carried off in the arms of a handsome prince (or, in my case, the arms of my best friend's brother). While some people – such as that aforementioned best friend – might say that this fantasy is the result of an impressionable young mind warped by too many viewings of *Ever After* or *The Slipper and the Rose*, and that in this day and age it shows a terrifying lack of feminist empowerment, I'm here to tell you that just because you've married someone who happens to be royal, rich and famous doesn't mean you have given up in your quest for self-actualization! Look at the examples of the some of the following women, all of whom became princesses after marrying the man they loved, and tell me if you think they've lost their grip on their own identity!

Grace Kelly

By Tina Hakim Baba, High-School Romance Expert and Daughter of a Supermodel and an Arab Sheikh [with commentary by Mia Thermopolis]

Grace Kelly was this totally beautiful movie star in the fifties who was rich and famous in her own right when she went to the small principality of

Monaco to film a movie called *To Catch a Thief*. While she was there, she met the Prince of Monaco (being a principality much like Genovia, Monaco is ruled by a prince or princess instead of a king or queen).

Prince Rainier was instantly smitten by Grace's beauty and charm, and asked her to be his bride. Grace agreed, and while it's true that she never made another movie again, you have to ask yourself: would you? I mean, if you'd found your handsome prince at last, would you keep slogging away at the acting thing, constantly having to watch what you eat so you can squeeze into the tiny dresses inflicted on you by the costume department, and eating stale tuna-fish sandwiches from Craft Services? When you could lounge around by the pool in a kaftan and eat all the Häagen-Dazs you wanted?

I thought as much.

Grace Kelly and Prince Rainier had three kids together. You can read about two of them on pages 36—38. The third one, Prince Albert, was (the last time I heard) still available and looking for his own princess. But I haven't given Tina his email address because he is too old for her. And besides, she is saving herself for Prince William.

Tina's Random Act of Princess:

Be like Grace: wear large dark glasses and a filmy scarf over your hair next time you go out in public. People will totally wonder who the mysterious beauty is standing in line behind them at Blockbuster.

Diana, Princess of Wales

Lady Diana Spencer was just a shy girl of nineteen when she agreed to marry Prince Charles, the heir to the British throne, who was twelve years her senior. But she soon overcame that shyness, blossoming into one of the most beautiful women in the world, becoming a fashion trendsetter and a muse for designers such as Bill Blass and Valentino. She also became a spokeswoman for causes such as landmine reform, which seeks to remove unexploded landmines from war-torn areas such as Chad, and AIDS. Diana was, in fact, the first member of the British royal family to publicly embrace an HIV-positive hospital patient.

While sadly, Charles and Diana's marriage didn't last, they remained fiercely supportive of their sons, Princes William and Harry, two of the finest-looking male specimens ever to walk the planet, and one of whom I am going to marry, if there is any justice at all in this world.

I have explained and explained to Tina, until I was blue in the face, practically, that being a princess is not all it's cracked up to be. But will she listen? No. I have also pointed out that even if she does marry William, she will never be Queen, because she is not a British citizen and doesn't even know what toad-in-the-hole is. She says she doesn't care, when William is king he can change the rules to make her Queen if he wants to.

She does have a point there. And better Queen Tina than Queen Britney, is all I have to say. Although, of course, I secretly like Britney, so I wouldn't actually mind her being Queen. In fact, it would be kind of cool. Especially, you know, if she wore short-shorts to Ascot.

Tina's Random Act of Princess:

Be like Diana: adopt a cause about which you feel strongly. Educate your friends about it, and enlist their support as well. Remember, to think globally, you have to act locally. Every little bit helps. (PS You might meet cute guys this way, if you pick a cause boys like, such as one involving comic books or video games.)

Queen Noor

Queen Noor was born Lisa Najeeb Halaby. She didn't become a royal until she married King Hussein of Jordan in 1978. Since then, Queen Noor has worked hard to address issues of education, women and children's welfare, human rights, environmental and architectural conservation and urban planning, not just in Jordan but, working with the UN, globally as well. Queen Noor is active in trying to combat 'honour killings' in Jordan where girls' fathers or brothers kill them (!!!!) for 'shaming' the family in ways that here in America would not even  raise an eyebrow, such as going to the movies with a boy or whatever. Queen Noor is my total role model and when I grow up I want to be just like her. Except I want hair like Shakira's.

Plus, Queen Noor manages to do all this while looking like a model. Not that looking like a model is so important. Except that it helps spread the word about your causes when you just happen to be stylish enough to be on the cover of 'Vogue'.

Tina's Random Act of Princess:

Be like Noor: you don't have to wear combat boots or pierce parts of your face to show that you are part of the counterculture. It's even more subversive to try to look as polished and professional as you can, and just when people are lulled into a false sense of complacency, hit them with your cool plan for raising awareness of the plight of the sea turtle, or whatever.

Cinderella

Everybody knows the story of Cinderella, the poor 'cinder wench' who was forced by her evil stepmother to clean the chimney hearth rather than attend a palace ball. Cindy got her own back, though, by summoning a fairy godmother who outfitted her in glass slippers (maybe not the wisest choice in footwear, but pretty!) and a coach made out of a pumpkin. Then off Cindy went, in her glass shoes and harvest-vegetable transport, to the palace, where she won the heart of the

prince she would eventually marry, after he tracked her down again (via the glass shoe)!

It would be crazy to think Cinderella missed her chimney-cleaning days. Of course she loved living in the palace, and I'll bet anything she and the prince became a much-beloved king and queen. If that's not happily ever after, I don't know what is.

In the Disney version of this story, talking mice and birds help Cinderella make her dress for the ball, and she forgives both her stepmother and her stepsisters in the end. In the original version by the Brothers Grimm, however, those birds peck out the eyes of the evil stepmother and stepsisters. Wouldn't it have been AWESOME if they'd included that in the Disney version? Not that I can stand the sight of blood . . . even cartoon blood. Still, it would have been cool to watch, you know, while the credits were rolling, or whatever.

Tina's Random Act of Princess:

Be like Cindy: you too can be the belle of the ball! Instead of shopping for your next prom dress at the local mall, try a vintage clothing store, or your local thrift shop. Not only can you find great bargains, but you can be assured that no one will be wearing your exact same dress! You will be a true original.

Beauty from *Beauty and the Beast*

The daughter of non-royals, Beauty (or Belle, which means 'beautiful' in French) is a bookish but undeniably attractive girl who offers to go in her father's place when a hideous monster threatens to keep him captive in an enchanted castle. For her self-sacrifice, Belle is rewarded with her life, which the monster spares. She gets to hang out in this beautiful palace, with all these new clothes that fit perfectly, and read romance novels all day. Enchanted kitchenware even brings her her meals! She never even has to get up . . . except maybe when the Beast asks her to dance, which he does, frequently. Everything is going along just great, when Belle gets a vision that her dad is in trouble, and she has to go back home and save him. Poor Beast nearly dies of loneliness without her. Plus a whole bunch of mean villagers come along and want to kill him (in the Disney version).

Fortunately Belle comes back to the enchanted castle and confesses her love for the

Beast and kisses him and breaks the spell. He stops being a Beast, and turns back into a handsome prince.* You just know that he and Belle are happy together for the rest of their lives, because they've both learned what it's like to almost lose the thing you hold most dear in the whole world. **

* This is the worst part of the whole story, if you ask me. Why couldn't he have stayed a beast? It is always so disappointing when the Beast turns into the Prince, because who wants a smoothie Prince when you can have a big hairy Beast? That's like choosing Cyclops over Wolverine, and who in their right mind would do that (except for Jean Grey)? Anyway, the whole thing ends up being a pretty raw deal for Belle, if you ask me.

** In spite of my dissatisfaction with the way it ends, this is the best fairy tale of all time. Lilly says it is based on the old Greek myth of Cupid and Psyche, or possibly the Roman myth of Persephone and Hades, and that its subtext is all about S-E-X. I don't care what it's based on or what the subtext is. It RULES. The Beast is SO HOT — especially when he is bossing Belle around, and she stands up to him

like the little spitfire she is. That is SO like me and Michael. I mean like completely.

Tina's Random Act of Princess:

Be like Belle: give that ugly guy in your Bio class a second look. Yeah, he might tuck his sweater into his pants and wear a retainer . . . but when he takes it out, he might be a totally excellent kisser! It's just like Mrs Potts says: there might be something there that wasn't there before.

Clarisse, Dowager Princess of Genovia

Clarisse Renaldo, née Grimaldi, was just a carefree young debutante – educated in the finest finishing schools in Europe, and garbed in only the most flattering creations of top designers of the era, such as Givenchy and Dior – when she caught the

eye of the handsome Prince of Genovia one night at a ball given in his honour. Instantly smitten, the Prince pursued Clarisse relentlessly, but she would have nothing to do with him, for Clarisse had aspirations of her own, and they had nothing to do with wife and motherhood. No, Clarisse, though she had never admitted as much to her staid mother and father, wanted a career . . . a career on the stage! Not since Sarah

Bernhardt had the world seen such an actress as Clarisse . . . or so she had been assured by all her finishing-school chums, after she starred as Yum-Yum in the school's version of *The Mikado*.

It was only when Clarisse's mother pointed out that in order to be an actress, Clarisse would have to move to America, most specifically Hollywood, that the young princess-to-be knew her dream would never be realized . . . because while Clarisse would gladly live in Paris or New York, nothing in the world would ever induce her to move to Los Angeles. And so she accepted the young prince's proposal, and became Genovia's most beautiful and charismatic – princess of all time.

I can't believe Grandmere managed to weasel her way into this section. And that she convinced Tina she wanted to be an actress. She told ME she wanted to be a brain surgeon.

Tina's Random Act of Princess:

Be like Clarisse: go to the animal shelter and adopt a small stray dog. Take it with you everywhere dogs are allowed. In places where dogs are not allowed, take your canine friend anyway, hidden in a large chic purse.

v. Power Princesses

Princesses Who Wielded a Heavy Sceptre

A Note from Princess Mia

Sad but true: some of the world's greatest leaders have been overlooked by historians, simply because they happened to have been born lacking a Y chromosome! Look at Lady Jane Grey: she was Queen of England until she was beheaded for treason*, but does anybody ever hear about Queen Jane? No! Even the movie they made about her was called *Lady Jane*.

---

* *I am so totally glad that there's no death penalty in Genovia. It would fully suck to be beheaded for not doing my job well. I mean, think about that whole thing with the parking meters . . . sheesh. People can be so touchy.*

And OK, maybe it's because Jane was only queen for nine days, and that's not a whole lot of time to make sweeping social change. But they could still give the girl her props. I mean, she was a *queen*!

I'm just saying, we hear a lot about the men who ruled the throne, but not so much about the ladies. So here are some women who ruled not only wisely, but well, and what we can learn from their triumphs, as well as their mistakes.

Cleopatra

By Lilly Moscovitz, Best Friend to Princess Mia, and Writer, Producer and Director of Lilly Tells It Like It Is.
[with commentary by Mia Thermopolis]

The last of the Egyptian monarchs, before Egypt was overtaken by the Romans, Cleopatra is perhaps best known for her memorable introduction to Julius Caesar. Always one to make a big impression, Cleo arrived at Julius's house rolled up in a carpet, from which she was dramatically unrolled by Nubian slaves. In this way, Cleopatra was a lot like one of our modern-day pop princesses, Britney Spears, who once showed up at the MTV Video Music Awards wearing very little but a five-foot banana snake around her neck.

It is doubtful, however, that Britney could have manipulated her boyfriends as skilfully as Cleopatra did (I mean, look at how messy her break up with Justin turned out). Cleopatra's relationship with Marc Anthony (after she dumped Julius) kept her, for many years, the most powerful woman in the world.

What is not generally remembered about the Queen of the Nile was her fluency in nine languages, her skill at mathematics and military strategy and her devotion to her country. Her profile graced the coins of not just Egypt, but the Roman denarii as well, and circulated throughout the Mediterranean. It is unlikely the same will ever be said of Britney. Cleopatra truly was, as  she considered herself, the New Isis, achieving in death by asp – Cleopatra chose to take her own life rather than become enslaved by her enemies – certain immortality, according to the Egyptian religion.

An asp, for those of you who don't get 'Animal Planet', is a poisonous snake. And how cool would it be if money had Britney Spears's picture on it? Like if Britney were on the five-dollar bill? That would make buying things so much more fun!

Although really, if you think about it, Cleopatra is

more like the J-Lo of the ancient world. I mean, J-Lo's likeness is on just about as much stuff. Let's just hope her luck with boys turns out better, you know, than poor Cleo's.

Lilly's Random Act of Princess:

Be like Cleo: make a big entrance at YOUR next party or school event. You don't have to roll yourself up in a carpet (dusty and impractical). But you CAN stride confidently through the doors as if you own the place. Soon people will be looking up to YOU as the Queen of the Nile.

Eleanor of Aquitaine

Though she married, at the age of fifteen, King Louis VII of France, wealthy and intelligent Eleanor of Aquitaine wasn't content to sit at home embroidering tapestries. When the Second Crusade rolled around, Eleanor dressed up in waiting in armour and lances and, with three hundred of her ladies-in-waiting in attendance, descended upon the city of Antioch, where she pledged to help with the wounded.

A military strategist at heart, Eleanor disagreed with her husband's objective of reaching Jerusalem. This is not unlike my own mother, who frequently disagrees with my father when he opts to take the 130 instead of the Turnpike when we are headed to the Jersey shore for a weekend of familial bonding. Unlike my mother, however, when Eleanor's husband, as she predicted, failed to reach his goal, she got the church to end their marriage by granting her an annulment. My own mother just gloats.

Eleanor enjoyed immense fame throughout Europe for having made popular the idea of the 'art of courtly love' – proper courting techniques, which she insisted the knights of her court used whilst wooing their ladies. Her second husband, Henry, who was not exactly faithful, could have used some lessons in the art of courtly love . . . it might have spared him his wife leading his own children in a rebellion against him, causing Henry to imprison her for fifteen years . . . much like what Donald Trump did to Ivana over the whole Marla Maples thing. Only Ivana's prison was the Plaza.

Don't worry, though. Eleanor got her revenge on all her enemies by outliving them and dying at a ripe old age, a very rich, very happy old lady.

One thing Eleanor made popular in her court was picking lice out of your lover's hair, then putting them in a locket and wearing it around your neck, as sort of proof that you were allowed close enough to the owner of the lice to pick them from their hair. I kid you not. Thank God today we just use Sticky cameras.

Mia's Random Act of Princess:

Be like Eleanor: compose a love sonnet dedicated to the object of your affections. You probably shouldn't show it to him, though. He might run from you like a startled fawn, frightened by the strength of your ardour.

Princess Ariel

Contrary to what Mia thinks, I don't mean Princess Ariel, the mermaid: I mean Thundarr the Barbarian's friend – or possibly girlfriend. We will probably never know the true status of Ariel and Thundarr's relationship, because this excellent animated series was cancelled in its prime. Also I don't believe either Thundarr or Ariel was really all that into labelling their relationship – you know, boyfriend/girlfriend versus just friends. Ariel was too busy travelling around post-apocalyptic earth in a sparkly unitard, helping Thundarr and his mutant friend Ukla right wrongs done by evil warlords, and Thundarr was . . . well, too busy being Thundarr.

Ariel wasn't just a princess, either. She was a sorceress too, who had special magic bracelets that aided her in correcting the deviant behaviour of evil-doers (too bad the NYPD can't get their hands on a pair of those). The power source for these bracelets has long been a source of debate amongst fans of the 'toon. However, intensive research (a Thundarr marathon on the Cartoon Network) reveals that the bracelets were most likely powered by some force within Ariel herself. Whether her sorcery was Wiccan in origin, or perhaps something she came across while rooting through some old twenty-first-century stuff – an old Tony Robbins video, like *Power Talk* perhaps will probably remain a mystery forever . . . which of course only makes Princess Ariel more compelling. "Ariel! Ukla! Ride!"

Plus, you know, seeing as how a comet had split the moon in half, causing Armageddon back on earth, Ariel was the last princess on the planet. It was a LOT of responsibility. Credit to her for dealing with it so bravely, and for all that running around, even when she had her period and probably wanted to do nothing more than curl up with a copy of 'Cosmo' and a cup of Swiss Miss fat-free cocoa with mini-marshmallows.

Mia's Random Act of Princess:

Be like Ariel: buy a necklace, ring or bracelet (or use one you already own) as your personal talisman, and wear it every single day. If people ask you why you wear it, look mysterious and don't answer. Soon the object will take on mystical properties and give you power beyond your imagination. Or not.

Elizabeth the First

The Virgin Queen (although if you believe the Cate Blanchett movie made about her, she wasn't as virginal as all that) gave her name to what was arguably the most colourful and magnificent era in English history. It is interesting that a woman whose father had his own wife – Elizabeth's mother, Anne Boleyn – beheaded would prove to be such a level-headed and effective leader. One would have thought Elizabeth would at least have developed a borderline personality disorder or antisocial tendencies at the very least, but she managed not to fall into the trap of victimhood and grew up with only a firm resolve never to marry (who can blame her?).

The Elizabethan Age brought with it not just a renaissance in art and music, but also Philip Sidney, Francis Drake, Walter Raleigh and, of course, the Bard himself, William Shakespeare. England's Golden Age took place during the latter part of Elizabeth's reign. Francis Bacon was one of the Queen's lawyers, and Edmund Spenser wrote *The Faerie Queene* in her honour during this time. Although the Queen often hinted she would marry in order to form pacts and allegiances with other countries, she never did, and while some might find the reluctance of one of the most powerful women in the world to marry neurotic, I find her aversion to the matrimonial state understandable, given the example set by her own parents' marriage.

And of course — perhaps most compelling of all — Elizabethan England was the backdrop for one of the most important cultural events of our time . . . the movie 'Shakespeare in Love'! Which proved flat-chested girls can get guys too!!!!! And who can forget Dame Judi Dench's portrayal of Elizabeth the First, in her stiff collar and white face paint (face paint that, it was later revealed, was lead-based, causing the skin of her face to peel and crack — Queen Elizabeth's, not Dame Judi Dench's)? And what about all those scenes where Will had his shirt off? Two thumbs way up for Queen Elizabeth!

Lilly's Random Act of Princess:

Be like Elizabeth I: write and then perform a one-woman play about you and your closest friends. Invite them to see it. Serve refreshments afterwards, to ward off any hard feelings.

Aura

Queen Elizabeth the First was not the only royal with a pronounced Electra complex. Princess Aura, the daughter of Ming the Merciless (better known as Flash Gordon's mortal enemy) spent most of her time – pre-arrival of Flash – in the palace lounging around in sparkly halter-neck tops, trying to get her dad's attention. But when your father is the ruler of the entire galaxy, how much quality time, really, can you expect him to spend with his offspring – especially when he has, at the last count, over sixty wives?

If you think about it, what happened next was all Ming's fault. If he had just given Aura the unconditional love she so craved, she might never have turned on him. But Ming was so busy thinking up ways to thwart that meddling earthman Flash Gordon that he didn't notice the rebellion rising up in his own household . . . not until it was far, far too late. Aura joined forces with Flash and his dashingly handsome friend the Baron (who represented a father figure to her, perhaps????) and took part in the battle that ultimately resulted in Ming being ousted from power and his eventual death. Aura proved to be a thoughtful and responsible leader, treating all her father's former subjects with respect, even his wives.

As if it wasn't bad enough that her dad wanted nothing to do with her, Aura also had this total crush on Flash Gordon — who her dad was always trying to kill, by the way, and who liked this other chick, Dale Arden, the whole time. Worse, Ming even tried to make Dale his sixty-first wife, just to get under Flash's skin. How mental would you go if your dad tried to marry the girl-friend of the guy you had a crush on? Think about it. It's a wonder Aura never went space happy and shot up the entire Imperial household.

Lilly's Random Act of Princess:

Be like Aura: take your dad or other important male figure in your life to lunch. Let him know how important he is to you. Tell him you will always be there for him. Later that day, ask him if you can borrow ten dollars. If you've played your cards right, it will work! Spend your hard-earned money on candy or cosmetics.

Isabella the First

A daughter of John II of England, Isabella I of Spain wasn't going to let any man tell her what to do, particularly her own brother, which, given the fact that she ruled during the 1400s, a time when women throughout the world were pretty much treated as chattels and second-class citizens, was pretty daring. Isabella married who she wanted to – Ferdinand of Portugal, who became King of Aragon – and did what she wanted to with her money – funded Christopher Columbus's trip to the New World.

But being ruler of the newly reunited Spain (she had Castile and he had Aragon, which was essentially Spain) wasn't all fun and paella. Isabella was

also at least partly responsible, along with her husband, for the Spanish Inquisition, during which time anybody who wasn't Christian got expelled from her country – including Jews and Muslims – or worse, burnt at the stake.

Still, Isabella had her soft side as well. She was an educated woman who was known as a patron of scholars and artists. And when Christopher Columbus brought to Spain some of the Native Americans he'd captured in the New World, Isabella insisted they be returned to their native land and set free. In her will, she stipulated that the people of the land Columbus had discovered be treated with justice and fairness.

Too bad nobody paid any attention.

When I take over the throne of Genovia, I will so never launch any sort of Inquisition. Well, maybe a little one, but just to root out anybody who wears fur who isn't an Eskimo and doesn't believe animals have rights too.

Lilly's Random Act of Princess:

Be like Isabella: shower your enemies with unconditional love. Say 'Good morning' to the girls who hate you the most. When they mock you, smile sweetly – but pityingly – at them. Do this enough times and they will become confused and wary of you. It really works!

Adora

Known to most as She-Ra, Princess of Power, Adora resides in the fictional world of Etheria. She-Ra, as everyone knows, is the sister of He-Man, who abides in a place called Eternia. It is typical that the creators of this animated classic, who were likely male, used the Latin root 'eth', as in ethereal, or dreamlike and unreal, for their female protagonist's planet, while the male protagonist got to live in a place that sounds like eternal, or eternity – going on forever.

But why quibble? She-Ra was still a pretty dope heroine, fighting to protect the magical Crystal Castle against her evil foes. Whenever her services were needed, the Princess would raise her 'Sword of Protection' in the air and shout, 'For the honour of Greyskull!' Obvious phallic representation aside, this is still pretty cool.

Even though She-Ra will be known through-out cartoon history as 'He-Man's sister', she was also a strong female who was able to succeed without the help of any male authority figures. Still, the poor thing doubtlessly suffered from the severest form of sibling rivalry, as who would not envy the popularity of her brother, He-Man, par-ticularly amongst pre-adolescent boys?

All I know is, my She-Ra action figure was too short to go out with Ken, and too tall for Han Solo, and He-Man was her brother, so who was she supposed to go out with? WHO????

Mia's Random Act of Princess:

Be like She-Ra: invent your own magical king-dom. Before you go to sleep at night, imagine what it looks like, and who else lives there. Make sure one of its inhabitants is a hot guy who totally adores you and lives to do your bidding. Whenever

you feel down, pretend this guy is sitting next to you, telling you how cool he thinks you are. Then make out with him. (PS If a real boy asks you out, don't say no just because he isn't as hot as your make-believe boyfriend. That would just be stupid.)

VI. Action Princesses

Princesses Who Kicked Butt, Royal and Otherwise

A Note from Princess Mia Thermopolis

While I'm not exactly an authority on the whole princess thing, I can totally attest to the fact that there have been – and still are some kick-ass princesses out there whose stories definitely deserve to be told.

A lot of people seem to be under the impression that all princesses are good for is pricking their fingers on things or modelling the latest styles from some new designer. Nothing could be further from the truth! There are lots of princesses who have ruled over their people with fairness and wisdom, making far more effective leaders than their less even-tempered fathers, brothers or husbands.

And more than one of them has, in her quest to provide her people with proper government, taken up a sword or laser pistol to ensure that things turned out her way. It's princesses like these who make it less revolting for me to admit that royal blood courses through my veins.

Now if I could just convince my dad to let me have a flame-thrower . . .

Boadicea

By Michael Moscovitz, Boyfriend Slash Royal Consort
to Princess Mia Thermopolis
with commentary by Mia Thermopolis

Things were rough in 61BC. The Romans were pretty much running the show, notably in Great Britain, where they weren't too popular . . .

especially when the Iceni King Prasutagus died, leaving his wealth and kingdom to his wife, Boadicea, and his two daughters, Princesses Camorra and Tosca, and the Romans refused to recognize the Celtic law that allowed females to inherit.

Big mistake. When the local Romans attempted to take over Iceni property, Boadicea and her daughters joined another Celtic tribe, and marched on London, burning down the entire city and killing 20,000 Roman soldiers along the way.

By the time the Romans finally sent enough re-inforcements to beat Boadicea, her army stood at 80,000 strong. Boadicea, rather than admit defeat, took poison. But monuments to her bravery exist in England to this day. A modern representation of her famous scythe-wheeled chariot (shades of James Bond's tricked-out Aston Martin here?) can be seen at the end of Westminster Bridge, and Boadicea herself is said to buried beneath what is now Platform Ten of King's Cross Railway Station.

I don't believe I will be taking poison if, say, Monaco ever tries to take Genovia from me. I mean, instead I will try to find peaceful methods of resolution. But I could totally use a scythe-wheeled chariot. To ride in during the next school pep rally, perhaps.

Michael's Random Act of Princess:

Be like Boadicea: don't stand by and let the unpopular kids in your school get picked on. Take a stand and defend them. You'll not only make new friends, but you might also find yourself elected to a position on the student government.

Matilda

Perhaps one of the least known of the English monarchs, the Empress Matilda reigned as Domina, or Lady of the English, for six months during the year 1141. Due to a disagreement with her cousin Stephen over just who, exactly, had the right to the throne, a civil war broke out, with half of Europe backing Matilda, and the other half backing her cousin. The war got so bad, that people went around saying that all the saints and angels must be sleeping, and that's why they didn't lift a finger to stop the two warring royals.

When Stephen finally captured his cousin and locked her in Oxford Castle, Matilda didn't just meekly accept it. Instead, she waited until the dead of night, then, dressed entirely in white, climbed down a rope from one of the castle's windows, and fled across the frozen river Isis, undetectable in her robes that matched the

colour of the snow. Stephen won the war and went on to rule England for a dozen more years, but Matilda got the last laugh, outliving him by more than a decade.

If my cousin Prince René ever tried to snake the Genovian throne out from under me, you can bet I'd fight him too. For one thing, I wouldn't want to see Genovia turned into a giant party town, like New Orleans. And for another, he has absolutely no concern for the marine life in the port.

Mia's Random Act of Princess:

Be like Matilda: a bit of white by the face can brighten any complexion (just ask Judge Judy). Throw on a white turtleneck or scarf, then sit back and wait for the compliments.

Xena, Warrior Princess

Xena's history is a complicated one, and is cloaked in a patina of sorrow. Xena started out as a warlord, killing all who stood in the way of her quest for total world domination. By the time she eventually saw the error of her ways, she had cut a swathe of terror across the land that caused many to tremble at the mere mention of her name (kind of the way Pavlov trembles when he hears the voice of my sister, Lilly, only for different reasons*).

*Lilly insists she is totally sorry for what she did to Pavlov. I was with her at the time and can testify that she fully outfitted Michael's sheltie in one of those plastic foot-ball helmets from Dairy Queen before she put him in that suitcase and swung him around over her head a few times. Besides, as

soon as I saw what she was doing, I made her stop. She swears it was just an experiment having to do with the laws of gravity, and Pavlov, when I let him out of the suitcase, was totally fine . . . it just took the room a few minutes to stop spinning around for him.

However, Xena was truly sorry for the horrific acts she'd done (unlike my sister), and reformed herself, starting to fight instead for the rights of the less fortunate, vanquishing those who preyed upon the weak, and sometimes using gravity-defying martial manoeuvres while doing so. Xena and her sidekick, Gabrielle, ride around, seeking out injustice so they can right it, while wearing . . . well, not a lot of clothes. It is just wrong that this fine, fine show was cancelled.

Michael's Random Act of Princess:

Be like Xena: do something nice for your best friend, such as agree to see the lame romantic comedy she's been dying to go to, instead of the cool action flick you've been waiting for. She'll appreciate you all the more, and you'll be filled with a warm, fuzzy feeling because you were so selfless.

Pocahontas

Pocahontas may not have had an adorable pet raccoon in real life, like she does in the Disney movie, but she was a real princess. She did meet and marry a man named John, just like in the movie – except that he wasn't the John she threw herself in front of in order to save him from the wrath of the Powhatans. That was Captain John Smith. Pocahontas instead married the other John, whose last name was Rolfe. He taught her English, and she taught him her native language. Eventually, she went with him back to England, where she enjoyed immense popularity and was treated as what she was . . . visiting royalty.

Until, that is, she got smallpox, and died at the age of twenty-two.

Whoa! That last part is so not in the movie version! What a bummer!

Michael's Random Act of Princess:

Be like Pocahontas: learn a foreign language! It will come in handy when you're meeting with dignitaries from foreign lands, or at least look good on your college apps.

Wonder Woman

Princess Diana of Paradise Island was raised by her mother, Hippolyte, Queen of the Amazons, in a place devoid of the war-embracing ways of men. Until, that is, World War II pilot Steve Trevor's plane is shot down, and his unconscious body washes up on Paradise Island's virgin shores. Princess Diana is instantly smitten, so when Steve's wounds have healed enough for him to be moved, she volunteers to take him back to his people.

In order to prepare her daughter for the dangers the Queen knows she'll face in the land of men, Hippolyte gives Diana a golden lasso, which compels whoever holds it to tell the truth, and she also loans her the royal invisible jet (don't even ask how an island of Amazons who haven't had any contact with the outside world developed the technology to build an invisible jet. You wouldn't believe me if I told you).

Armed with these things and a pair of wrist bracelets with which Diana can ward off bullets, the young Amazon princess heads for Washington DC, a groggy Steve in tow. There, Diana is appalled by all the evil she sees – and not  just from the Nazis. She vows to remain by Steve's side, to protect him as best she can from those who seek to kill him, which actually turns out to be a lot of people. Like *Superman's* Lois Lane, Steve never quite figures out that his mild-mannered secretary, Diana, and Wonder Woman, the Amazonian princess who keeps stopping all the bank robberies in the Washington area, are one and the same person.

Like Diana, I too would go to whatever lengths I had to to make sure my man was safe from the Nazi scourge . . . even if that meant forsaking my native land and running around our nation's capital in nothing but a one-piece bathing suit with gold eagle wings where the built-in bra shelf should have been. I would gladly make such a sacrifice, if it would in any way aid my love.

Mia's Random Act of Princess:

Be like Wonder Woman: wear your bathing suit proudly. Don't slouch or try to look inconspicuous, no matter how big you think your thighs are, or how little you've got going in the chest area. Anyone can look good at the beach or pool, if she's got the most important accessory of all: confidence.

Princess Leia

Leia Organa, adopted daughter of Bail Organa, Viceroy of the doomed planet of Alderaan, has a complicated, and some would say convoluted, family tree. Her birth mother (see pages 116–117) split up Leia and her twin brother at a young age, opting to raise Leia until her own death.

Leia was a born leader, and became a senator at a very young age, striving to help her people, whom she saw as oppressed by the Imperial government. An active member in the Rebellion against the galaxian ruler Emperor Palpatine, Leia little expected to be captured and held a political prisoner by a man who would later turn out to be her own father . . . or that she would be rescued by a man who later turned out to be her own brother. Or that she would fall in love with a smuggler with a heart of gold, and later be forced to wear a slave-girl outfit while serving drinks to that same smuggler's mortal enemy, Jabba the Hutt—

I had to cut Michael off here. His thing on Princess Leia went on and on! Who knew there was so much to say about her?

Mia's Random Act of Princess:

Be like Leia: experiment with new hairstyles! You'll never know what looks good on you until you've tried a lot of different looks. Who knows? Maybe the real you is all about buns on the side of your head! Even if you do something as radical as shaving off all your hair, or dying it pink, no worries: the great thing about hair is, it grows back!

Queen Amidala, or Padmé, Princess Leia's Mother

Padmé Amidala was elected queen of her planet at the age of fourteen. Some might say it was unwise of the people of her planet to elect such a young queen. To them I say . . . didn't you see her in *Attack of the Clones*? She looked totally hot in that white pantsuit. I mean . . . what I meant to say was Queen Amidala served her term on the throne and later became a senator, serving her people wisely and well, until that Hayden Christensen guy came along and messed it all up—

I had to cut Michael off AGAIN! He was getting kind of wound up . . . the same way he gets about Buffy the Vampire Slayer, only worse.

116

Mia's Random Act of Princess:

Be like Padmé: don't wear whatever style is 'in' just because everyone else is doing it. Find what looks best on you, whether it's long and flowing or sporty and form-fitting. Don't let the in-crowd dictate what goes on your body. Choose the look that you feel comfortable – and look good – in.

Princess Amelia Mignonette Grimaldi Thermopolis Renaldo

Mia Thermopolis, also known as Princess Amelia Renaldo, only recently became heir to the throne of her native land, Genovia, but has already made great strides in rectifying many social problems affecting the tiny nation, including the crippling parking problem there (by implementing parking meters). Mia has also cleaned up the Port of Genovia and lessened the incidences of sea mammals getting their snouts caught in plastic six-pack holders by almost sixty per cent.

Mia continues to show great promise in

an area which used to trouble her greatly . . . Algebra. She is funny and smart and, though she doesn't necessarily agree, is also totally gorgeous, and looks great no matter what she's got on, overalls or ball gown. Plus her kindness and generosity to others knows no bounds. Which is why I love her.

!!!!!!!!!!!!!!!!!!!!!!

I swear I didn't tell him to write that!

MM + MT = TRUE LOVE
4-EVER!!

Michael's Random Act of Princess:

Be like Mia: don't drop litter or smoke, and try to walk, ride your bike or take public transportation instead of burning more of our precious natural resources. And spit your gum out in the nearest trash receptacle: birds can be attracted to the colour if you spit it on the ground, and eat your gum and get their beaks stuck shut and starve to death.

VII. Politically-Correct Princesses

Princesses Who Taught Us Valuable Lessons

By Mia Thermopolis

For some reason writers seem to think that if they throw a princess into a story, people will pay more attention to it. This must explain why there is such a plethora of princesses in fairy tales, which were originally conceived (back in the days before the Cartoon Network and *Seventh Heaven*) to warn kids about the dangers of modern-day society.

But since these stories were written in the year 1200 or whatever, and modern-day society was like a cluster of thatched cottages protected by a feudal lord, instead of warning the kids to say no to drugs and not get into cars with strangers, the warnings are all about the dangers of trading the family cow for magic beans or stealing cabbages from the local witch's garden.

Still, considering the fact that most of them were written a millennium ago, these stories have some staying power . . . I mean, they are still around. And, personally, while I don't see the appeal of using royalty as a vehicle to propel your narration – I mean, who cares if the person playing with the spindle is a princess or just your average serf? The message is the same: use caution when handling sharp objects! – I guess it *does* make the story more memorable or whatever.

Here are a few of my favourite PC princesses, in no particular order.

Princess Lily in the Movie *Legend*

Princess Lily (played by the luminous Mia Sara) has a problem: she is in love with Tom Cruise, who in the movie plays some kind of elf or something – I was never too clear on just what, exactly, Tom is supposed to be. Anyway, Lily aka Mia (ha!) throws this ring into the river and tells Tom if he finds it he can marry her (which if you ask me is being way demanding, even for a princess. I mean, guys are scared enough of commitment without us making things even more complicated by forcing them to go deep-sea diving for our engagement rings. But whatever). While Tom is under water looking around for the ring, some kind of troll-like thing who looks a bit like Satan takes over the kingdom (it could happen), because he is in love with Mia Sara too (who wouldn't be?).

The thing is, everything would have been OK if Mia had listened to Tom and stayed away from the unicorns. But no, she had to go and pet one and, well, there's this whole thing about how virgins are the only ones who can catch unicorns, which is like this legend from King Arthur's days, which Lilly says is totally sexist and that the unicorn's horn is this phallic symbol and that you shouldn't like them because if you do it means you want to touch boys' you-know-whats, but whatever. The POINT IS (get it???) because Mia Sara touched the unicorn, Satan Troll's henchmen were able to trap it and drag it and Mia to their underground lair, where Mia was forced to dance around in a tacky black dress

124

that looks like the one Cher wore when she won the Oscar for *Moonstruck*. After a lot of networking with dwarfs and fairies and a couple of deadly battles, Tom is finally able to save the day and put things back as they were.

But none of it would have happened if Mia hadn't thrown that stupid ring into the river. So the moral of the story is: don't try to force guys to perform over-the-top feats of athleticism to prove their love for you. Be happy with what you have.

Mia's Random Act of Princess:

Be like Lily: admire the pretty unicorns from afar, but for God's sake, DON'T TOUCH THEM!!!!!!!!!!!

The Frog Princess

OK, so there was this princess and she was all snotty because she had all this long, shimmery, blonde hair and a perfect body and all the guys in the kingdom were in love with her and she was captain of the junior varsity cheerleading squad . . .

Oh no, wait. That's somebody else.

Anyway, this princess was all perfect and stuff and so one day when she was playing with her golden ball (whatever . . . just go with it. Golden balls are what princesses used to play with before there were Game Boys) and it fell into the royal pond, she was way bummed out, because nothing bad like that had ever happened to her before. Obviously HER dad never made her take

Algebra. But whatever.

So when this big, ugly frog hopped out of the pond and was all, 'I'll get you your ball back if you kiss me,' the princess was like, 'Ew, gross, no way,' because kissing a frog has got to be even worse than kissing a mouth-breather who wears a bionater and can't stop tucking his sweater into his pants . . .

Oh no, wait. That's somebody else.

But the princess really wanted her ball back, so she told the frog she'd kiss him, and like a schmuck he went and gave her her ball back before making her follow through on her end of the dealio, which if you ask me is like paying the cab driver BEFORE he gets to the airport, but whatever. Anyway, the princess was so

overjoyed to have her stupid ball back she ran away (no big surprise). Well, the poor frog really had no choice but to hop in and interrupt the royal dinner that night and tell the King how his daughter wouldn't keep her word. The King was understandably embarrassed (although if a frog hopped into the dining room at the Palais de Genovia and started talking, embarrassed would not be the word to describe my dad's reaction) and told the princess she had to kiss the frog. The princess was pretty grossed out by this but she had no choice: she kissed the frog.

And of course the minute her lips touched the frog's, he turned into a prince, who was not only good-looking, but also willing to marry her on the spot, which if you ask me is the most unbelievable thing in the whole story, because, hello, it took some of us like eight years to get our handsome princes even to ask us out, let alone propose, but whatever.

The moral of the story is: don't judge amphibians by how they look.

Mia's Random Act of Princess:

Be like the Frog Princess: if you've done something wrong, don't make up excuses: just apologize. And then don't do it again! People – even princes – will respect you for it.

Snow White

There's no point in even going into this one, since you all know it so well. I mean, some of us even had Snow White birthday cakes when we turned six, and dressed like her for Hallowe'en four years in a row, and memorized all the songs from the movie and went around singing 'Someday My Prince Will Come' until our mothers threatened to buy us *Free To Be You and Me*, so we'd learn that it is both inappropriate and unwise in today's day and age to wait for princes to come rescue us . . .

Mia's Random Act of Princess:

Be like Snow White: don't take fruit from strangers. This includes ones you meet over the Internet. Sure, they SEEM nice, but you never know if that guy claiming to be a Justin Timberlake lookalike might actually be an evil queen out to destroy you.

Princess Mononoke

Princess Mononoke, a character in a Japanese anime movie of the same name, grew up in a forest populated by animal gods, and was herself raised by the Wolf God. When a young prince is infected by an incurable disease thanks to the bite of a Boar God, he travels to the forest in the hope of throwing himself upon the mercy of the all-powerful Deer God, who might be able to save him. When he gets there, however, he finds San (aka Princess Mononoke), who is more than a little hostile towards him thanks to the encroachment of man – in the form of a nearby ironworks

 – upon her forest. The ironworks is slowly exploiting and killing the forest dwellers, and Princess Mononoke is determined to put a stop to it . . . even if it means killing her own kind.

Princess Mononoke is the avenging angel of the environment, and I can't help wishing that, instead of being Princess of Genovia, I were princess of the forest she lives in, and that, instead of Grandmere, the Deer God was my mentor in all things royal.

But that probably wouldn't work out, because Fat Louie is really more of an indoor cat, and I don't know how long he'd last outside, due to his weight problem and addiction to Tender Vittles, which I don't think you can get in the woods.

Mia's Random Act of Princess:

Be like Mononoke: keep your local parks and nature preserves pollution-free and litter-free. Your animal friends will thank you. Probably not by rushing to your rescue if you find yourself imperilled in the woods or anything. But you never know. And it certainly can't hurt.

Princess Aurora, aka Sleeping Beauty

The Princess Aurora got into trouble for something that wasn't even her fault: her parents 'forgot' to invite the wicked angel to her christening (kind of like my mom 'forgot' to invite her parents to her wedding to Mr Gianini – thankfully Grandmere remembered for her). The evil fairy was pretty peeved about the whole thing, and so laid a curse on poor Princess Aurora, saying that on her sixteenth birthday she would prick her finger on a spinning wheel and die (fairy curses were way harsh back then).

Well, this other fairy tried to soften the blow by amending the curse so that, instead of dying, Princess Aurora would just sleep for a hundred years, but, as you can imagine, her parents were not comforted. They banished all the spinning wheels from the kingdom – which begs the question, what did they wear for the next sixteen years? Because without spinning wheels, nobody was making any clothes. It wasn't like they could just mosey on over to the Gap.

Well, anyway, yada yada yada, Princess Aurora managed to find a spindle somehow, and of course she touched it, and slipped into a coma, and if you go by the Disney version, so did everybody else in the castle, and if you go by the original version, everybody else just died, and Aurora slept for a hundred years until this prince came along and laid a big wet one on her kisser. Which of course can only make one question the prince's motivation: I mean, do YOU kiss every sleeping person YOU happen upon? But maybe he was lulled into it by her cherry lips or something.

Anyway, Aurora woke up, and so did the rest of the castle, and she and the prince turned out to have a lot in common or something, because they got married and lived happily ever after.

The moral of the story is, not surprisingly: DON'T TOUCH SPINDLES!

Mia's Random Act of Princess:

Be like Aurora: embrace, not alienate, your relatives. You never know when they might put a curse on your offspring! Instead, just PRETEND to like them. You won't be sorry, even if they don't turn out to be evil fairies.

VIII. Wanna-Be Princesses

People Who Are Not Princesses But Are Often Mistaken for Them

By Mia Thermopolis

Let's face it: there are a lot of princesses out there. It can get confusing sometimes, trying to figure out who is really a princess versus who just acts like one. Hopefully this little chart will help clear things up.

Gwyneth Paltrow

Looks like a princess, dresses like a princess, has possibly played princesses in movies, and has even dated a prince, but Gwyneth is not, as of this writing, technically a princess.

Britney Spears

Frequently referred to as a pop princess, Britney did briefly exchange emails with Prince William, but that does not make her a princess.

Christina Aguilera

Ditto, minus the Prince William part.

Barbie

A lot of people think Barbie is a princess, but, the truth is, Barbie only DRESSES like a princess. She is not actually the ruler of Mattel, any more than she is actually a flight attendant, Olympic figure skater, veterinarian, nurse, school teacher, lawyer, doctor, space-shuttle pilot, dog groomer or cheerleader.

Although she does have some of the best princess clothes I have ever seen.

Alice Roosevelt

Dubbed Princess Alice by the press, the daughter of President Theodore Roosevelt was not, in fact, a princess. Still, you have to give her credit for having her own car at a time when most people in America were still driving horse-and-buggies.

Mulan

Listed by Disney as one of their many princesses, Mulan is, in fact, a commoner, and remains one even after marriage, since that hot soldier dude she marries isn't royal either. Sorry.

Sara Crewe, of *A Little Princess*

She acts with the nobility and grace of a royal, but Sara Crewe never actually became a princess through the whole of the Frances Hodgson Burnett book about her. Still very much worth reading, though.

Smurfette

Even though Smurfette was the only female Smurf in the kingdom, she was not its princess. Smurfs appeared to have formed an early democratic society, over which Papa Smurf, in all his wisdom, presided.

Grandmere's sisters,
Tante Simone and Tante Jean-Marie

Much as they might like us to believe the contrary, Grandmere's sisters are not actually princesses. They are in fact distant cousins – as is Grandmere – to the royal family of Monaco. However, they certainly *act* like princesses, particularly in the whining category.

Strawberry Shortcake

Not a princess. OK?

IX. Should-Be Princesses

People Who Should Be Princesses But Aren't

By Mia Thermopolis

There are any number of people in this world who, through some trick of fate, ended up not being princesses when, by rights, they really should have been. If we could elect our princesses, instead of them having to be born or to marry into the title, I would nominate the following women, for their joie de vivre, their chutzpah, and their generally princess-like behaviour:

Gwen Stefani

For writing the song 'I'm Just A Girl', which so plaintively points out the pitfalls of being born female in American society today, and for being such a good role model to aspiring teen rockers everywhere, and also for looking so pretty on her wedding day.

Elizabeth Taylor

For her work on behalf of people living with AIDS – not to mention her excellent work in the film *National Velvet* – 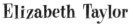 Elizabeth Taylor truly deserves to be an HRH.

Buffy the Vampire Slayer

She kills vampires. Need I say more? OK, well, she guarded the Hellmouth in Sunnydale, California, keeping the world from apocalypse, totally sacrificing any hope of a social life. Once she even had to kill her own boyfriend because he'd turned evil and was going to unleash hell on earth. If that is not worthy of princessdom, I don't know what is.

Powerpuff Girls

The Powerpuff Girls – Blossom, Buttercup and Bubbles – were made by accident in a laboratory. On the outside they look like ordinary little girls, but, inside, they have special powers that give them superhuman strength and enable them to fly. They use their powers for good, not evil, and should be named honorary princesses, if anyone should.

Lara Croft

Um, hello, the whole bungee cord thing. Not to mention her accent. Come on. This is prime princess stuff.

Chelsea Clinton

She grew up in the White House; was First Daughter throughout her formative teen years; never got arrested or made any other embarrassing social gaffes; never stopped speaking to her parents even when they might have deserved it, and hangs out with Madonna. This girl already IS a princess.

Julie Andrews

Julie Andrews isn't a princess, although she has played them in movies (well, OK, a queen, anyway). She's entertained us for many years with her portrayals of magical nannies, musical governesses and cockney flower-sellers. Ever gracious and good humoured, Ms Andrews truly deserves to be addressed as Her Royal Highness. We already know she looks good in a crown.

Lisa Simpson

The voice of reason in the Simpson family, Lisa is the smartest second-grader on the planet. Maybe she isn't the most popular girl in her school, but she is definitely who I'd want to be trapped with on a desert island, because she'd figure out a way to get off in no time. Plus she loves animals and the environment – perfect princess material! And, with her spiky hair, it already looks like she's got a built-in tiara anyway.

YOU

Because who deserves it more? I mean, you know now that all it takes to be a princess (besides a country to rule) is kindness, confidence, observation of proper hygiene, generosity with your time and consciousness of the environment . . . everything, really, that makes a model human being. Because in the end, that's all princesses really are: human beings, just like you. Only they happen to come with a crown.

X. Conclusion

Getting In Touch With Your Inner Princess

By Mia Thermopolis

Learning about the lives of other princesses has really helped me put things in perspective . . . like when I have a term paper due on the life cycle of the ice-worm on the same day as I'm expected to deliver an address at the UN, and my hair is looking particularly triangular-shaped and I spilt hoisin sauce on my lap, I can just be all, 'Well, this isn't really so bad, because look what Princess Aura, the daughter of Ming the Merciless, had to put up with,' and so on.

And it all just sort of falls into place.

Because the truth is, whatever your problems are, there is probably a princess somewhere in history or literature who has dealt with it before you, from whom you can learn valuable coping techniques. By following their examples, and incorporating 'random acts of princess' into your daily life, you will not only be better prepared for your turn on the throne (should you ever happen to inherit one), but you will be that much closer to achieving self-actualization.

Because though it is true we are all unique and special individuals – like snowflakes, only, you know, bigger and not frozen – there is one thing we all have in common:

We think princesses rule.

And by applying what princesses have taught us into your daily life, so can you!

MEG CABOT

The Princess Diaries Diary 2005

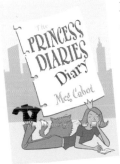

Keep your very own Princess Diary! A fun and funky diary where you can record the intimate details of your secret crush and make your own Top Ten List of Ultimate Hotties! Princess Mia herself has made several entries too. Just make sure you don't miss a single day. After all, you never know when your real parents may show up to crown you!

MEG CABOT

The Princess Diaries Guide to Life

Discover your inner princess!

Have you always wanted to be a princess? Ever checked for a pea under your mattress? While you're waiting to ascend the throne, let Princess Mia and her very special guests tell you what's what about being royalty. It includes a guide to the right royal wardrobe and an insight into the mysterious world of guys – whether princely or not.

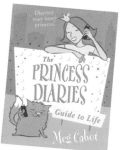

MEG CABOT

Funny, romantic and totally sassy, the first two books in
The Mediator *series will chill you . . . and thrill you!*

THE MEDIATOR I: Dead Gorgeous

Susannah Simon is a mediator – someone who eases the path
of the unhappy dead into the afterlife. A pretty tough job for a
sixteen-year-old. Luckily Suze is ready to kick some serious
ghost butt if she has to.

Just moved to California, Suze's mediator skills are put to
the test when a particularly nasty spirit is hell-bent on making
her life a misery. At least she's sharing her new room with Jesse,
who just happens to be *the* most gorgeous ghost in history.
But can Suze win the heart of the sexiest
spook in town?

THE MEDIATOR II: High Stakes

Susannah Simon's new life in California is pretty cool.
There's the pool parties, the new friends, and the fact that
the hottest ghost in history just happens to live in her bedroom.

But when a screaming spirit appears at the end of her
bed, Suze is soon on the trail of a murderer. All the clues
lead to the totally weird father of Tad Beaumont, the cutest
boy in school . . . and the only guy who's ever asked Suze
out. Things are about to get very complicated . . .

MEG CABOT

All American Girl

Just as a general thing, when you have saved the life of the leader of the free world, most people really want to hear about that and, sadly, don't care to hear a long-winded description of your dog.

Sam Madison's life used to be simple – if boring. After all, it's not much fun being the totally forgotten middle sister between a perfect, beautiful older one (Lucy) and a genius, precocious younger one (Rebecca). And then there's the weird art class Sam's been made to attend. Er, hello, what is *that* all about?

But then comes the day that changes everything – when Sam stops a crazy psycho from assassinating the President of the United States and becomes an instant, world-famous, full-on celebrity. Dining at the White House sure isn't easy for someone who only eats hamburgers and fries, and who lives in combat boots.

In fact, there's only one compensation – David, the President's son . . .

Two totally frivolous, deliciously frothy,
tongue-in-cheek romances

MEG CABOT

Nicola and the Viscount

Nicola is in love! And not just with an ordinary man. Her heart has been captured by Lord Sebastian, better known as The God – the most handsome and dashing man who ever lived.

But are gods always quite as perfect as they are meant to be? Nicola is about to find out . . .

MEG CABOT

Victoria and the Rogue

Lady Victoria Arbuthnot has always done exactly what she wants. So she's delighted when she bags drop-dead-gorgeous Lord Malfrey before she's even got off the boat from India. But then a dashing young sea captain starts spreading stories about her man. Could it be that Vicky's happy-ever-after with Lord M. might not be so happy after all?